For my brilliant, wonderful and brave friend Ileana . . .
the most CAN BE Chameleon I know.

—C. F.

Published by Yeehoo Press
721 W Whittier Blvd, Suite O, La Habra, CA 90631
www.yeehoopress.com

The illustrations for this book were created in Photoshop.
This book was edited by Rebecca Frazer and designed by Mei Yanya.

Library of Congress Control Number: 2021930622
ISBN: 978-1-953458-15-5
Printed in China First Edition
1 2 3 4 5 6 7 8 9 10

CHAMELEON

CAN BE

By Carolina Farías

YEEHOO
PRESS

In a forest filled with trees,
Nestled between twigs and leaves,
A beautiful flower grew
In a bright yellow hue!

But look very closely and see
Among the frogs, bugs, and bees,
The beautiful flower of yellow
Is really me—a camouflaged fellow!

I want to be someone new
And see life from a different view.
So, I wonder what I will be
If I'm someone other than me!

After thinking all day and all night,
An idea sprung to mind like a light.

Dazzling is how I want to be!
Do you think you can help me?

YES, WE CAN!!

I'll hold leaves like a wing I can flap.
Fan them like feathers, I'm one dapper chap!
Everyone will travel to see.
I'm a magnificent bird . . .
What could I be?

A peacock!

No, peacock actually doesn't feel right.

I want to go on adventures that are grand
And fly above sand, shells, and land!
I'll swoop down to catch fish in the sea.
I have a big beak . . . What could I be?

I want to be curious and explore
And find bananas on the rainforest's floor.
I will swing from vines in the trees.
I'll have a long, hairy tail . . . What could I be?

A monkey!

No, monkey actually doesn't feel right.

I want to be powerful from my head to my toes
And have a horn on the tip of my nose.
I will charge in a mighty stampede.
I'll have a big, giant body . . . What could I be?

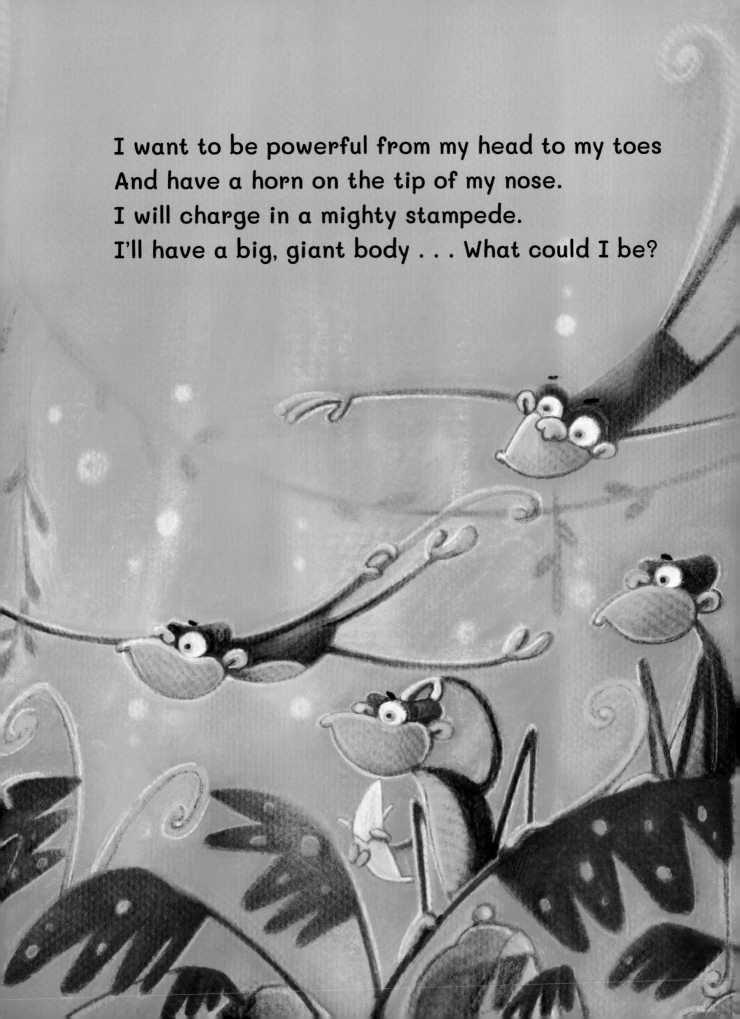

I want to be fierce and live in the ocean.
I will swim in the most graceful motion.
When I flash my sharp teeth, all will flee.
I'll be an all-mighty fish . . .
What could I be?

A shark!

No, shark actually doesn't feel right.

I want to be fluffy and gray
And sleep all night and all day.
I will munch on eucalyptus leaves.
I'll be a cuddly bear . . . What could I be?

RRR

A lion!

No, lion actually doesn't feel right.

I tried a little and a lot,
But I don't want to be something I'm not.

I want to be colorful—red, green, yellow, and blue,
And to myself I want to be true.
I am good at hiding and live in a tree.
I'm a master of disguise . . .

What could I be?

A chameleon!

I thought changing was actually
quite clever. But being me——
I'm the happiest chameleon ever.

So, when I ask, "What could I be?"
The answer will always be . . .

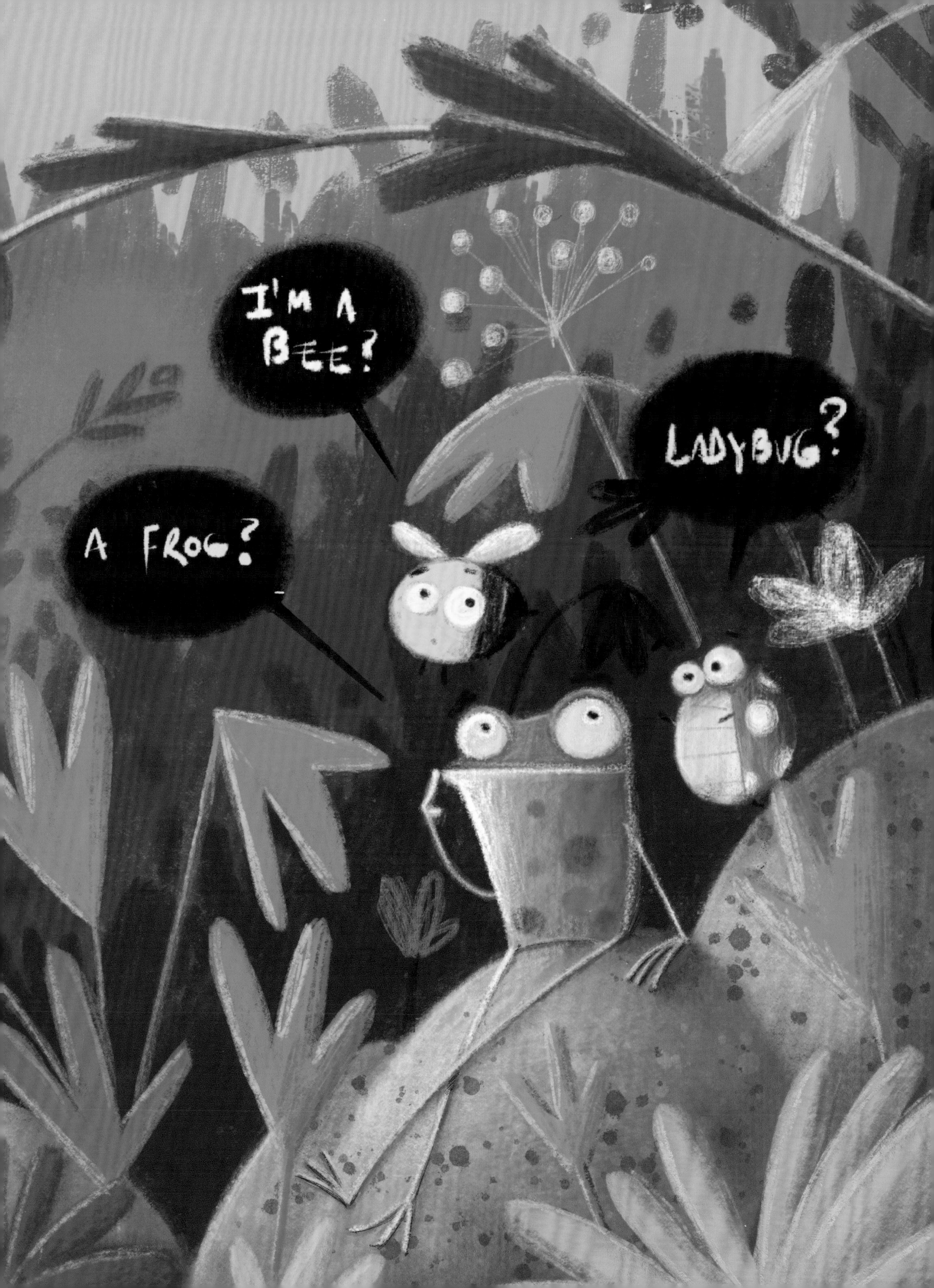
I'M A BEE?
A FROG?
LADYBUG?